The Monster in the Mountains

by
Anne Schraff

•

Perfection Learning Corporation
Logan, Iowa 51546

Cover Illustration: Michael Aspengren

For more information, contact:
Perfection Learning Corporation
1000 North Second Avenue, P.O. Box 500,
Logan, Iowa 51546-0500.
Tel: 1-800-831-4190 • Fax: 1-712-644-2392

Paperback ISBN 0-7891-5517-6
Cover Craft® ISBN 0-7569-0229-1
perfectionlearning.com
Printed in the U.S.A.
5 6 7 PP 08 07 06

1 "Can you believe we start camp in just a week?" 18-year-old Carmela Masters asked her two friends. It was the week after graduation, and the friends were lounging around at Carmela's house.

"I know it," said Jeff Lyman, also a recent graduate of Cleveland High. "I haven't even thought about packing yet."

Carmela, Jeff, and Lauren Woodham had started as junior counselors at the middle school camp three years earlier. Junior counselors helped run errands and set up activities and meals. Senior counselors supervised a group of campers.

"Wow, we'll have our own group of campers this year," commented Lauren.

"Yeah," said Carmela, "we'll be in charge of all the activities—hiking, fishing, crafts . . ."

"You're forgetting something," said Lauren. "What's the highlight of the week for the kids?"

"Man, I almost forgot," said Jeff, realizing what Lauren was talking about. "The big scare!"

"Oh, yeah!" Carmela said. "But how are we going to top last year's?"

It was a tradition at camp that each year the senior counselors would dream up a scary hoax to play on the kids. The counselors would think of some fun way to scare the living daylights out of them.

Last year one of the counselors had dressed up as Bigfoot, the legendary mountain creature. Bigfoot stumbled into camp, growling and knocking over everything. The kids didn't stop talking about Bigfoot for the rest of the camp.

"We can't do Bigfoot again," Lauren said. "Too many of the campers will have heard all about it."

"What if one of us dressed up as a ghost?" Jeff suggested.

Both Carmela and Lauren laughed at that suggestion. "Like with a white sheet and eyeholes cut out?" Lauren asked. "Oh, that is so incredibly lame. The kids would just laugh at us."

"Yeah," Carmela said. "Every year it

gets harder. When I went to Camp Roadrunner as a sixth-grader, the counselors just played this scary ghost music, and everyone freaked out. But kids today see so many more scary movies and stuff on the Internet that it takes a lot more to scare them."

"You're right," Jeff agreed. "We've got to think of something different. It's got to be more realistic."

"I know!" Lauren cried suddenly. "I remember reading about some old hermit who used to live in the mountains around the camp. I think his name was Don Clay. Anyway, he was really angry when the land around him started to be developed. I think he died, but we could pretend like he had come out of the grave to harass us. We could dress one of us up in ghoulish makeup, like a dead person walking . . ."

"Hey, that's got possibilities," Carmela said. "We could kind of prepare the kids by telling them how upset this guy was when people came into the mountains and bothered the bears and stuff. Then this horrible creature would come along, sort of like a walking skeleton."

"I don't know," Jeff said. "Do you think that'll be too much? I mean, I don't want the camp directors to freak out and fire us."

"Oh, Jeff," Lauren laughed, "we're not going to get fired. We all know Ms. Lawson and Mr. Webb would never approve of anything we came up with. But then when it's all over and the kids are laughing and hugging one another and talking about what happened, Lawson and Webb will just be happy that the campers got a thrill."

Carmela nodded her head in agreement.

"Look," Lauren continued, "it's not like we're doing anything dangerous. The kids will be gathered around the fire for a ghost story, and this horrible creature will just come staggering from the woods."

"Yeah," Carmela said, growing more excited as she thought about the idea. "It can happen just before it's time for the kids to go to bed."

"Oh, cool!" Lauren said. "This will be the best hoax ever. It's our last year as counselors, so I want to go out with a bang. I have a cousin who does special effects for TV. I'll email him and see if we can borrow a mask and makeup from him."

"Who's gonna play the monster?" Jeff asked.

Both girls turned to Jeff and grinned.

"No way," Jeff said. "Not me."

"Come on, Jeff," Carmela said, "be a good sport. Guys make better monsters than girls. Especially walking dead monsters. I bet we can find you the perfect clothes at Goodwill." She smiled sweetly. She knew they could talk him into it.

Jeff looked at his two friends who were batting their eyelashes at him. Carmela could tell it was working. He was giving in.

Jeff grimaced. "Oh, okay, I guess. But don't blame me if we get in trouble over this. I don't see why we can't just scare the kids with recorded coyote howls or something," he said.

Lauren burst out laughing. "Coyote howls! Come on, Jeff! Why don't we just try to scare them with a gorilla hand puppet?" she asked.

"Or we could get a really mean-looking teddy bear and have it fall from a tree," Carmela suggested, laughing.

"Okay, okay," Jeff grumbled, "you made your point. I'll do my best to pull this off. I'll tell you one thing, though. If I'd known how weird you guys were, I never would have volunteered to be on your counselor team!"

Carmela and Lauren laughed again. Jeff was a nice guy and a good friend. Carmela had been interested in going out with him in the past, but she had never pursued it. She didn't know how it would affect their friendship, and she didn't know how it would go over with Lauren, either.

Very few guys seemed interested in Lauren. She was a big, athletic girl with a loud, domineering voice. She wasn't petite and pretty like Carmela. Lauren never came right out and said she was hurt when guys didn't ask her out, but Carmela felt bad about it. She knew that deep down Lauren was hurting, and that hurt Carmela too because the girls had been best friends since fourth grade.

"Well, I'd better get home," Jeff said,

pulling himself up off the couch. "Are you guys going out tonight?"

Lauren looked at Carmela. "We hadn't talked about it yet," she said. "What do you think, Carmela? Do you want to go out and then spend the night at my house?"

"Sure, sounds fun," Carmela said. She loved staying at her best friend's house. Even though the two girls had been best friends for years, their lives were very different. Carmela lived in a very modest neighborhood. It seemed her parents were always trying to pull themselves up out of debt. Lauren's parents were wealthy, and Carmela loved staying at their plush home. She envied Lauren, who never had to want for anything.

2 When Carmela got home from Lauren's the next day, she decided she should start packing. "I'll help," her mom offered, following her daughter up the stairs to her room. As Carmela was packing T-shirts, shorts, swimsuits, and hiking shoes, her mom sat on the bed and sighed.

"You know, it's never been hard for me to send you off to camp," she told her daughter. "But for some reason, it's really getting to me this year. It must be because I know that this is your last summer at home. You'll only have a couple weeks between camp and college. Time is flying by so fast."

"Yeah, Mom, I know," said Carmela. "It's just going to be you and Dad around the house. I can't believe I've graduated and am only a couple months away from college!"

"Don't get me wrong," said Carmela's mom. "I'm really happy you're going to be a senior counselor this year. All that fresh air and exercise is good for you. And the experience will look good on your resumé. I'll just miss you, that's all."

"I'll miss you and Dad too," said Carmela.

A couple of nights before Carmela left for camp, the Masters family had their favorite meal—homemade lasagna, garlic breadsticks, and spinach salad with homemade raspberry vinegarette dressing.

"I'm going to savor this," said Carmela. "Camp Roadrunner doesn't serve cuisine of this caliber. Let's see, I'd better get used to eating chicken nuggets, hot dogs, and sub sandwiches."

Carmela's dad smiled. "I still remember going to summer camp when I was a kid," he said. "You know what the best part always was? The counselors would tell us these chilling tales, and we'd be so scared we'd be afraid to go to sleep! We'd hear about the headless horseman—you know, the Sleepy Hollow story—and some classic horror stories. Good, shivery fun. I think I still have an old book full of ghost stories if you'd like to take it along, Carmela."

"Thanks, Dad," Carmela said, hiding a smile. "But we've got newer stories. And we've got some of our own tricks up our sleeves to give the kids a good scare."

Mrs. Masters' eyebrows went up.

Here it comes, Carmela thought. She should've thought before she spoke. Her mom always seemed to find something to worry about. Carmela could see that concerned look on her mom's face, a look she was used to seeing.

"What kind of tricks?" Carmela's mom asked. "I hope you're not doing anything dangerous. You know, those kids are just, what, 12? You don't want to upset them too much and give them nightmares."

"Oh, Mom!" Carmela said. "You don't have a clue! These kids are way more mature than you think!"

Carmela smiled inwardly. Poor Mom, she thought. She lives in her own little dream world sometimes. She doesn't see how the world and kids today are changing.

"It's okay," Carmela assured her mom.

"We won't do anything dangerous. Just good, clean fun."

"Well, just don't do anything you'll regret," her mom warned. "Because kids that age can be very sensitive."

"Yeah, Mom," Carmela said, excusing herself from the table. She climbed the stairs to her room and made sure she had all the essentials for surviving a summer at camp. The mountains would be filled with middle school-aged campers and teenaged counselors. She thought there might be some good-looking guy counselor from another school, and she wanted to look as good as possible in case an opportunity came along.

So Carmela packed her lip gloss, mascara, powder, nail polish, the shampoo that fought her hair's tendency to be frizzy, and the skin cream that warded off dryness.

Carmela knew she was very pretty. She didn't think she was arrogant about her appearance, but it did make her proud to know that she looked nice. She enjoyed the attention she got from guys.

As the day of departure for the mountain camp drew closer, Carmela got even more excited. She was looking forward to a summer of swimming, hiking, and playing games with the campers. Although some counselors were only working one or two camps, Carmela had signed up to work the whole summer. She was excited about meeting new counselors, especially guys. But she was even more eager about the hoax and how cool the younger kids would think it was.

The night before camp started, Carmela, Lauren, and Jeff got together for last-minute plans.

"Lauren, did you get the mask and the makeup from your cousin?" Carmela asked as the trio sat down around a large three-cheese pizza.

Lauren took a big bite from her pizza slice and nodded. "Yeah. I went up to see him yesterday. He gave me this incredible mask and all kinds of gunk to make it look like bones are poking through the skin," she said.

"Oooh, that's wonderful," Carmela said. She watched Lauren eat another slice of pizza. Carmela didn't say anything, but she thought to herself that Lauren had put on some extra weight, and it didn't look good. At least Carmela thought it didn't. Lauren had dropped out of the spirit club and taken up weightlifting last year, which Carmela thought was a really bad idea. She didn't think guys liked sweaty girls with big muscles.

Carmela was hungry for another slice of pizza, but she wouldn't take it for fear of adding a pound or two. It amazed her that Lauren was gobbling so much pizza and not giving her weight a thought. Carmela watched her own diet like a hawk, and when she stepped on the scales and discovered an extra pound, she really skimped on food the next day.

"I even rehearsed with Jeff," Lauren boasted. "We decided that while you're telling our kids ghost stories and leading up to the tale of Don Clay, I'll be helping Jeff with his costume and makeup. And then on cue, he'll come walking out of the woods, moaning and groaning. I'll come from another direction. I'll yell real loud, 'Oh, no! It's Don Clay! He must have escaped from his grave. Ohhh, he looks dead! Just like he crawled from the grave!' "

"Great," Carmela said. "What should I do then?"

"You just scream. Make it sound really convincing. And Jeff will keep coming closer and closer. He'll walk real stiff-legged, like a zombie! Of course we can ad lib as we go along . . ." Lauren said, gulping down some orange soda.

"When the kids are really freaking, then we'll let them know it's a hoax, right?" Carmela asked.

"Yeah," Lauren said. "Jeff will pull off his mask, and the kids will see it's just him."

"I hope we can really scare them," Carmela said. "My dad still remembers the ghost stories he heard at camp when he was a kid. And they were nothing compared to what we're planning. This is so much better than the Bigfoot hoax last year!"

***

Early the next day, Carmela, Lauren, and Jeff climbed onto one of the buses with other teenaged counselors and sixth-graders from many local middle schools. It was an hour's drive into the mountains. When they got there, they met with the adult directors who would be supervising the counselor teams.

Ms. Lawson gave the senior counselors a pep talk before assigning them to their campers. "You are all young adults. You'll be going off to college soon. You've all been thoroughly trained in our counselor program, and you are veterans of Camp Roadrunner. I *trust* everything will go very smoothly," she said.

Then the directors began calling out names. When the campers were called, they joined their assigned counselors.

Carmela and Lauren were assigned eight girls, and Jeff had five boys. They were all wearing the official Camp Roadrunner uniform—red T-shirts with a roadrunner embroidered on the front and black shorts.

Carmela surveyed her group, deciding they seemed like nice kids. She had taken the counseling job because she enjoyed working with children. In fact, she planned to study elementary education in college. Although she really liked kids, she was glad to see that there didn't seem to be a whiny, homesick kid in the group, like one girl last year who cried for the whole week.

Lila was a tall, athletic girl, and Dawna was a quiet little blonde with glasses. Kiley was the smallest, and Kandace was the biggest and most spirited. The twins, Nina and Tina, were chatterboxes, and Gayla reminded Carmela of herself at that age, mature and pretty. The group was rounded out by Judy, a petite Asian girl.

"We're gonna have a lot of fun," Carmela said. The girls all cheered, even Dawna. Carmela hoped they were ready to get the most out of camp.

After the directors made some opening remarks about what to expect during the week, Carmela and Lauren took their group to the barracks to put away their belongings. Then the girls changed into their swimsuits. Since it was so unseasonably hot, the adults decided to scrap the usual outside "icebreaker" games and instead take the campers swimming.

After walking to Camp Roadrunner's beautiful Olympic-sized pool, the campers were eager to cool off. They ran and dove into the deep end. Carmela splashed in the pool with her charges, but Lauren decided to keep her T-shirt on and patrol around the pool. Carmela figured Lauren was not as eager as Carmela to show off her swimwear, especially since her thighs had expanded.

As Carmela swam around, she noticed another counselor standing by the pool overlooking the water. He was strikingly handsome. His tan skin glistened in the sun, and he had the bluest eyes Carmela had ever seen. Carmela didn't recognize him. She figured he must be from another high school. She knew he'd never worked at Camp Roadrunner before.

Carmela swam close to Lauren. Before she could say anything about the new guy, Lauren spoke up. "Carmela, did you see that guy over there?" she asked. "Is he the most gorgeous piece of work you've ever seen?" Lauren's eyes sparkled with interest.

Carmela nodded. "He's hot, all right," she said.

Then Carmela slipped out of the pool beside Lauren and squeezed her wet hair. She stood in the hot sunshine, toweling off the dampness. In a few seconds she noticed that the guy was staring at her.

"Do you have to preen like some stupid peacock every time a cute guy gets within a hundred feet of you?" Lauren asked sharply. Carmela was stunned by the bitter tone of her voice. Lauren had never said anything before about being jealous of Carmela. She never complained about Carmela's popularity.

"Lauren! I wasn't preening!" Carmela defended. "I'm not doing anything on purpose. I'm just drying off."

Lauren looked rueful. "I'm sorry," she said quickly. "I shouldn't have said that. I don't know why I said it."

Carmela looked at her best friend, almost with pity. Lauren *was* jealous. She had probably been jealous for a long time and had just hidden her feelings. A girl wasn't supposed to be jealous—especially of her best friend.

Poor Lauren, Carmela thought. She knew she wasn't as pretty as Carmela. But they were always together, and every time a cute guy showed up, Lauren had to feel overshadowed.

The good-looking counselor was walking closer now, his eyes fixed on Carmela. Lauren might as well have been a beach ball for all the interest he showed.

3 "Hi, I'm Vance Putnam," the boy said. He was smiling at Carmela.

"I'm Carmela Masters," Carmela said. Since Lauren was right next to her, she thought she'd better introduce her too. "This is my best friend, Lauren Woodham."

"Hi," Vance said to Lauren, the words sounding more like an obligation than a privilege. He immediately turned his attention back to Carmela.

Lauren spoke up quickly, almost desperately. "I'm just taking a month out of my summer to be here at Camp Roadrunner, but my heart is already in Acapulco. Mexico, you know. It's just so fabulous."

That was the one area where Lauren was way ahead of Carmela. Lauren was the only child of older, rich parents who doted on and indulged their daughter. She had already been to Europe four times, and the family spent their summers in a condo in Mexico.

"Acapulco?" Vance repeated, his eyes widening and an unbelieving grin on his face. "Your parents are letting you hang out in Acapulco for the summer?"

"Oh, we go every year," Lauren said. "We have a really beautiful condo down there. Sometimes I take friends from school along, and we have a blast. It's a huge condo, isn't it, Carmela? Carmela was there once."

"Yeah, it's fabulous," Carmela said. "It's air-conditioned and everything." That meant a lot to Carmela. The little wood and stucco house where she lived with her family was miserably hot in summer with only fans to cool it.

"Wow," Vance said, "you must be rich."

Lauren shrugged and said, "I guess we're pretty lucky. My parents can afford just about anything we want."

Lauren was flaunting her wealth, Carmela thought. She did that sometimes to impress people with whom she wanted to be friends. Carmela thought it was kind of sad, but she didn't say anything.

"Well," Vance said, "I'll see you two around this week." He walked away, leaving the girls alone.

Carmela remembered that summer she had gone with Lauren to Acapulco. It was an incredible experience. She thought it was very generous of Lauren to invite her, but afterwards Lauren seemed a little sorry she had done it. Carmela didn't understand why at the time, but now she did. There were a lot of cute local boys around the condos, and they all noticed Carmela, not Lauren. Carmela figured that Lauren must have been really frustrated.

"He seems nice," Lauren said as Vance hit the water with a group of middle school boys. Carmela hadn't formed any opinion about Vance yet. How much can you know about a person after such a short time? she wondered. All she knew about Vance was that he *was* really hot.

"Carmela," Lauren said, finally taking her eyes off the boy, "we need to get together with Jeff tonight and fine-tune our hoax. I think we should plan on doing it tomorrow night. After the marshmallow roast tonight, the three of us will have some free time. We're off duty for a while after lights-out. Other counselors are supposed to be covering our kids."

"OK," Carmela said. "Sounds good."

"We need to tell the kids all about this Don Clay guy, how he used to wander about yelling at campers who left trash around and how he got really strange just before he died. Maybe you could weave his story into the ghost stories you tell them tomorrow night," Lauren said.

"Yeah, then when they see this horrible guy coming out of the woods, they'll know it's him," Carmela said.

As Carmela sat on her beach towel, soaking in the sun, she looked around at the beautiful, towering mountains in the bright afternoon sunlight. Sunshine splashed on the fragrant pines, and the lake sparkled like diamonds. It was hard to imagine anything spooky about the place.

But when darkness fell and the wind whistled through the trees, Carmela knew it would be a whole different story. The kids would be sitting around the campfire with strange shadows dancing on their faces from the flames. The arrival of the monster would be perfectly timed!

In the late afternoon, Ms. Lawson entered the pool area, making her rounds. After talking with several other counselors, she walked up to where Carmela, Lauren, and Jeff were sitting on the edge of the pool, their legs dangled in the cool water. "How are you doing with your girls?" she asked Lauren and Carmela.

"Wonderful," Carmela said. "They're great kids."

"I've got five lively guys," Jeff said. "A couple can get pretty obnoxious, but they're all getting along great."

"Then everybody is happy?" Ms. Lawson asked. She was always very anxious to make the camp experience a happy one for the middle schoolers. As directors of Camp Roadrunner, Ms. Lawson and Mr. Webb wanted to make sure that all their customers were satisfied so kids kept coming back. So far the camp was very profitable, and Carmela knew that the directors wanted to keep it that way.

Supper was served in the mess hall, one

of the few buildings with air-conditioning. Carmela sighed as she picked up her plate of chicken nuggets, corn, and a brownie. She already missed her mom's cooking.

Supper was spent getting to know the kids better. Jeff had to quell a ketchup fight that erupted among his active boys. "Just a sign of things to come!" he told Lauren and Carmela.

After supper, the three counselors roasted marshmallows with the kids. They told stories about the area to get the kids ready for what would happen the next night.

"For years and years a guy named Jake worked a mine about 50 miles from here," Carmela said. "He never got any gold, even though he worked his fingers to the bone. Then he died, and other guys came to work the mine. They got lucky. They struck gold right away and got rich."

"Wow, that wasn't fair," Spencer, one of Jeff's boys, said.

"Listen," Carmela said, "one night when these really lucky miners were sitting around a campfire, just like we're doing now, counting their gold nuggets, they heard this strange rattling sound, like a bag of bones being shaken."

"I bet it was Jake's ghost," Gayla cried, her eyes shining.

"Well," Carmela said, "this rattling sound got closer and closer. When the miners looked into the darkness, they saw a skeleton walking toward them with a miner's lantern embedded in his chest and holding a big pickax."

Carmela stopped and looked at the campers as their eyes shone big and bright in the light of the fire.

Lauren continued the story. "The skeleton swung the ax, and the miners got so scared that they dropped their gold and ran for their lives. But the skeleton ran faster. The miners stopped and picked up rocks to throw at the skeleton, but it didn't do any good. Jake was dead, and he couldn't be hurt anymore."

"What happened?" Kandace demanded.

"Well, the ghost of Jake chased the miners so far from their claim that when they got back, all the gold was gone," Carmela said.

"Cool," Carlos, one of Jeff's boys, said.

Carmela had a moment's misgiving about tomorrow night's hoax. Maybe they shouldn't be trying to scare the kids with Jeff's monster, she thought. But then she thought about Halloween and how kids clamor to go through haunted houses with the goriest and most frightening special effects. Kids love being scared, she told herself. And tomorrow's hoax was harmless.

"You know, we have a spooky story right around here, near Camp Roadrunner," Lauren said.

"Wow, did a skeleton chase somebody around here?" Judy asked.

"No," Carmela said, "but there was this man named Don Clay. He was really angry that the wilderness was being disturbed by people, and he raised a lot of trouble. Eventually he died. But some people think he still walks around at night, yelling and mumbling."

"How did he die?" Gayle asked.

"Nobody knows," Lauren said.

"Maybe bears got him," Chase, another boy, suggested. Everybody giggled nervously at that theory.

"There really aren't any huge bears around here," Dawna pointed out. "And anyway, if something like that happened, they would have found his remains."

"Maybe he was chewed up a little, and he crawled away to die," another boy, Darius, said.

"Yeah," a third boy said, "maybe the bear chewed off his head, and now he's walking around looking for it!"

Nervous laughter spread among the kids.

"Okay, campers, time to hit the hay," Jeff announced.

Groans erupted among the 12-year-old crowd, but they all got up from the campfire and headed toward their barracks.

Lauren and Carmela got all the girls inside the cabin and into their sleeping bags. Jeff did the same with his boys. Then the trio met in the moonlight between the cabins to make final arrangements for tomorrow's hoax.

"I'm not so sure we should be going through with this," Jeff worried. "Even that stuff we told them about Don Clay seemed too real. The Bigfoot thing we did last year was better. It was kinda funny. But some guy who gets half-eaten by a bear and now stumbles around looking for his head, that's pretty freaky. I just wish we'd call it all off. I've got a really bad feeling . . ."

"Oh, Jeff," Lauren said, "it's gonna be great. All you've got to do is come walking out real stiff-legged, with your arms out in front of you." She pointed toward the woods.

"You come out next to that crooked pine," Lauren continued. "You walk toward the fire. Your cue is when Carmela suddenly stands up, looks in the direction of the crooked pine, and yells 'What's *that?*' "

"Yeah," Jeff muttered glumly.

"Then you just keep coming, grunting and yelling," Lauren said. "The kids will all be sitting around the campfire, but it'll be barely flickering because Carmela will have just put it almost completely out."

Suddenly, they stopped talking.

"Who's there?" Carmela asked, a little too much edge in her voice. She hated to admit she, too, was getting a little spooked with all the talk of ghosts and monsters.

A figure was walking toward them out of the darkness!

"It's just me," the voice said, and Vance came into view. He had come from the direction of his cabin at the other end of the camp.

"Man, it's hard getting those guys into bed," Vance said. "Some of them want to stay up all night, and they say their parents let them. And then the wildlife stories around the campfire bombed too."

Lauren laughed. "We tell our kids ghost stories," she said. "The kids like scary stories more than they like stories about birds and stuff. Right, Carmela?"

"Yeah," Carmela said, hoping that Lauren didn't say much more. Carmela didn't want an outsider to know about their plans for the upcoming hoax.

"Cool," Vance said. "I didn't think we were allowed to tell ghost stories. I thought the parents would complain."

"Oh, it's okay," Carmela said. "It's harmless."

"The kids are so desensitized, though," Vance complained. "They're not interested in any tame stuff. Like I was telling them about how the cougars live, and all they wanted to talk about was cougars eating people. They didn't want to know about their habitat or anything."

Lauren edged closer to Vance. Carmela could see that she really had a crush on the guy. "You seem really interested in wildlife," she said. "I bet you want to be a naturalist or a scientist or something. I bet you get good grades too," she said.

Vance shrugged. "I do okay. Nothing great. I'll probably end up like my old man, scrounging for pennies working in a factory. Like my dad is always saying, 'The rich get richer and the poor get poorer, but what are you gonna do about it?' " His gaze went over to Carmela, and his tone softened. "I hope I see more of you tomorrow."

Carmela flushed. She could see the anger flash in Lauren's eyes. Even telling Vance about her family's condo in Mexico had not distracted him from Carmela. Lauren looked furious, and it made Carmela feel really bad.

"I'll be pretty busy tomorrow with the girls," Carmela said, trying to sound disinterested.

"Well, I'll be looking for you," Vance said with a wink.

Jeff walked off with Vance then, talking about various problems with the boys.

"Well, I suppose we should get some rest too," Carmela said, trying to make conversation with Lauren, who still looked upset.

"Yup," Lauren replied curtly before walking off to the cabin and climbing into bed without another word.

***

The next morning all the kids went fishing in a well-stocked stream in the canyon. Carmela didn't really know why she was so nervous, but she'd had butterflies in her stomach all morning.

"I'm having lots of fun," Dawna said as Carmela helped her bait her hook. Carmela didn't like doing it, but it came with the job. She usually made her dad do it for her when they went fishing.

"I'm glad you're having a good time,"

Carmela said. Once again the hoax flashed through her mind. Hopefully Dawna and the others would still think camp was fun after the hoax was over . . .

Maybe it wasn't such a good idea to try to scare the kids, Carmela thought. Maybe Jeff was right. Maybe they'd all get in big trouble with Ms. Lawson and Mr. Webb. The counselors who pulled the traditional hoaxes never got in trouble, but maybe this one was taking it too far.

But it was too late to worry about it now. Everything was planned. It was good to go.

The campers and counselors ate lunch in a clearing not far from the fishing hole. As Carmela was handing her girls their sandwiches, chips, and sodas, she noticed Vance staring her way. She just gave him a quick half-smile and went back to her work. Lauren still wasn't being very friendly toward her. She didn't want to give her friend reason to get even more upset by talking to Vance.

After lunch, the campers were scheduled to go on a nature hike around the base of the mountains. The vigorous exercise took Carmela's mind off the hoax for a while. But before she knew it, it was getting dark. Time for the campfire and supper—and the hoax.

Carmela gathered the girls and boys from their group around their campfire. They ate roasted hot dogs slathered with mustard and pickle relish and drank sodas.

Then Carmela started telling ghost stories as they had planned. She tried to remember all those urban legends that had freaked her out when she was in middle school. There was the one about the killer in the backseat of a car, or the couple on a date who heard a radio report about an escaped killer with a hook for an arm. She tried to pick stories that weren't too gruesome or mature for her group.

While she was narrating the spooky tales, she kept watching the woods for Jeff to appear by the crooked pine tree. The moment she saw him, she planned to jump up and shout, "What's that?" That would be his cue to come bounding into the camp.

Carmela looked around nervously. She wondered where Lauren was. She was supposed to appear at the edge of the woods right about now. Carmela didn't want to be alone with 13 screaming preteens when the hoax began.

She started to sweat. What was going on? she wondered. For a moment she thought that maybe Lauren and Jeff had decided to call the whole thing off. And actually, that thought brought her a flood of relief.

But then, at the edge of the woods but not anywhere near the crooked pine tree, a dark, ragged form appeared. The face was gray-green and hideous, with skin hanging in folds from the bony face. It looked as if it were half-alive and half-dead. Long dark hair hung in bloody strands from the creature's exposed skull.

Carmela was frozen in fear. It wasn't Jeff! It couldn't be Jeff!

Could it?

Carmela was too terrified to yell her cue. And then the thing began running toward her and the children.

Carmela sucked in her breath. Terror clutched at her, making it difficult to breathe.

4 "Look!" screamed Dawna. "It's that guy, Don Clay," Spencer yelled. "He's coming to get us!"

"Like the skeleton who chased the gold miners!" yelled Carlos.

Pandemonium broke out. All the kids were screaming and running toward the cabins. They raced inside the girls' cabin, which was nearest the campfire.

"Jeff!" Carmela screamed at the advancing monster. "Stop it! It's over! Go away!"

The creature approached Carmela. Then it reached out and grabbed her hair, pulling it sharply.

"Jeff! You idiot!" Carmela cried. "Stop it! Go away!"

Suddenly another ghoulishly made-up figure appeared by the crooked pine tree. Carmela stood, stunned and completely confused. The first horrible creature vanished back into the woods. The second one stood there, as if confused. The kids were all gone. Nobody was left around the campfire.

"Jeff!" Carmela shouted to the figure by the pine tree.

"What's going on?" Jeff yelled back.

By this time, Ms. Lawson and Mr. Webb were on the scene, attracted by the shouts and screams. Some of the bolder kids were already outside the cabin looking around.

"It was a hoax, you guys," Carmela said. "It was a joke! That monster over by the trees is just Jeff."

"What in the world is going on?" Ms. Lawson asked sharply.

"It was just . . . a hoax . . . just a fun trick," Carmela stammered. "We, uh . . . told the kids a ghost story, and then we sorta wanted to dramatize it."

Ms. Lawson looked grim. Mr. Webb yelled at Jeff, "Get out of that ridiculous costume right now!"

"It was just a trick," Carmela went on. "Every year counselors do stuff like this, and the kids love it. It's harmless. We just wanted to give the kids a little thrill."

Carmela looked around desperately for

Lauren. Where was she? she wondered. Carmela didn't want to take all the heat by herself. Did Lauren chicken out and just disappear until the trouble was over?

Jeff yanked off his mask. He looked shamefaced. "I'm really sorry, Ms. Lawson, Mr. Webb. This was a really stupid idea. Really stupid." He glared at Carmela.

"Listen," Carmela said, still confused about what had happened, "there was another person dressed up in monster makeup before Jeff even appeared. That's who scared the kids. Who was *that?*"

"What are you talking about?" Ms. Lawson asked coldly.

"The other monster," Carmela said. "Surely I'm not the only one who saw it!"

While two adult counselors stayed with the campers in the cabin and assured them that the frightening creature they saw was only a teen counselor acting stupid, Carmela and Jeff had to go to the office to further explain what they had done. Lauren still had not shown up. Carmela couldn't imagine where she was, and she was getting worried.

"I'm sorry about everything," Carmela said. "We didn't mean any harm, but it *was* stupid. Now that I think about it, we never should have done it."

"Three of us hatched the idea— Carmela, me, and Lauren," Jeff admitted. "By the way, where is Lauren?"

"We have some of the adult staff members searching the camp for her right now," Ms. Lawson said. "No doubt she is so embarrassed at being a part of this ill-conceived scheme that she's hiding in the woods somewhere."

Carmela nodded. Lauren probably thought she'd get the major blame since it was her idea. But both Carmela and Jeff were willing to share the blame with her. After all, any one of them could have put a stop to it.

Carmela looked at Jeff, "You saw the other monster, didn't you, Jeff?"

"I didn't see anything," Jeff said. "I was waiting for my cue."

Ms. Lawson stared at Carmela. "You must stop making up tales, Carmela. You are in enough trouble already for your foolish and immature behavior!"

"I'm not making up anything, Ms. Lawson," Carmela insisted. "I really saw this other person made up like a monster—this horrible creature with a skeleton face."

"Enough!" Ms. Lawson shouted. "If you didn't have such a good record as a counselor here, Carmela, and if we weren't so short of help, you'd be packing your bags to go home right now. I want you both to return to your cabins and your duties. For the rest of the week, you are to act with responsibility, is that clear?"

"Yes, ma'am," Carmela said.

"Nothing like this will ever happen again," said Jeff.

As Carmela and Jeff walked through the darkness back to their cabins, Carmela said, "Where do you think Lauren went? She's gonna be in major trouble if she just ran off and called her parents to come get her."

"She helped me put on the mask and makeup, and then she took off a little ahead of me for the rendezvous," Jeff said. "Maybe she saw all the ruckus and just freaked out and ran. But Lauren isn't really that kind of a girl. She's too feisty. I'm a little bit worried. I hope she didn't trip and fall into a ravine or something . . ."

When they were almost to the cabins, Carmela stopped. She turned to Jeff. "You don't think that Lauren decided to play a bigger joke and put on that hideous makeup after she helped you get ready?" she asked. "You don't think that Lauren was the first monster I saw? You don't think that's what happened, do you?"

Jeff looked perplexed. "Why would she do that?" he asked. "I suppose it's possible, but why . . ."

"Yeah," Carmela said. "But *where* is she?"

Clouds floated across the moon, darkening the camp. Jeff suddenly grabbed Carmela's arm and said, "Maybe that monster you saw was the *real thing*."

"What do you mean, 'the real thing?' " Carmela gasped. "Are you crazy? We dreamed up that ghost story about Don Clay. The whole thing was a figment of our imaginations. Are you saying that there's a real monster out there?"

Jeff shrugged. "I don't know. All I know is that we shouldn't be messing around with stuff like this—half-dead, half-alive zombies wandering around," he said.

"Oh, so you're saying we brought a curse on ourselves, right?" Carmela asked.

"I don't know what I'm saying, Carmela. I just wish we never would've gotten into all this," Jeff said.

Carmela joined her campers in the cabin. They were all in their pajamas and in animated conversation about what had happened.

"Oh, the first one was so gross," Dawna said. "I could see bones in his face!"

"Ewww," Gayla giggled, "he looked like something dead that the cat dragged in."

"Girls," Carmela said, "it was all a hoax. It's probably better if we just forget about it."

"I saw it pull your hair, Carmela," Kandace said. "Did it hurt you? Were you scared?"

Carmela got chills when she recalled the unknown creature touching her.

"Ewww," Gayla said, "did it touch your skin, Carmela? That must've been creepy!"

"Where's Lauren?" Kiley asked suddenly.

"Yeah, did Lauren disappear?" Tina demanded. "Maybe the monster got her!"

"Lauren is fine," Carmela said nervously. "She'll be back soon."

Carmela went to the window and stared into the darkness. Everything looked so spooky. Carmela couldn't believe that Lauren wasn't here. Could she have been the first monster? And when the hoax went sour, did she just take off? Did she pull a disappearing act to attract Vance's attention?

How could Lauren have left the mountain? Carmela wondered. Only camp traffic came near Camp Roadrunner. She couldn't have caught a bus out! But she *could* have called her parents to come get her.

Carmela shuddered. What if Jeff's suggestion was true? Maybe that first horrible-looking creature was some evil person who lived in the mountains. Maybe he had snatched poor Lauren!

I should be out there looking for her, Carmela thought. She's my best friend.

If *I* were out there, Lauren would be looking for me. I know she would . . .

The girls crawled into their sleeping bags. Carmela got ready for bed too. She didn't know what else to do. Until this happened, Carmela hadn't even thought of double-checking the doors and windows to make sure they were locked. Now she checked them several times. The horrible thing that had run up to her and pulled her hair was out there somewhere . . .

5 After about 20 minutes in bed, Carmela heard a faint tapping on the window. She went rigid with fear. Her first thought was that the monster was at the window. He was trying to get into the cabin!

Luckily, the excitement of the evening had caused the girls to fall asleep quickly. None of them awoke to the sound. Carmela crept out of bed. She tiptoed to the window. But she couldn't make herself pull aside the curtain. If she saw the ghoulish face of the monster, she thought she might faint.

Carmela decided to call an adult counselor on the cabin phone. But then she heard a familiar voice outside.

"Carmela!" the voice cried.

Carmela stopped, stiffening. She ran to the window and yanked the curtain aside. Lauren's bloodied face looked back at her. "Lauren! What happened?" Carmela gasped.

Kandace asked sleepily, "Is something wrong?"

"No, no, just go back to sleep. Lauren came back and she wants to go to bed. Shhh," Carmela said.

"Let me in!" Lauren said shrilly from the other side of the glass. Carmela quickly made her way to the door and unlocked it. Lauren stumbled in. Her T-shirt was torn, and her jeans were ripped and muddy as if she had fallen into a creek or something.

"Lauren, where were you?" Carmela whispered. "What happened?"

"Oh, Carmela! I was headed to the campfire when all of a sudden this horrible creature grabbed me. At first I thought it was Jeff, and I yelled at him to stop. But then I realized it was somebody else. He started dragging me into the woods!" Lauren cried.

Carmela stared at her friend. She didn't know if she believed her or not. Lauren sure looked messy, but that would have been easy enough to fake. "Lauren, how did you get away from this thing? And why have you been gone so long?" Carmela asked.

"I kicked at the creature really hard. Finally it let go, and I ran and ran. I didn't know where I was, so I couldn't find my way back to camp. Finally I found a cave near a little creek. I crawled in, and I tore my shirt on some berry bushes and ripped up my knee. I was so scared . . ." Lauren said. "I hid in the little cave until I was sure the thing was gone. I think it was looking for me."

"Oh, my gosh," Carmela said.

"Carmela, this is the most horrible thing that's ever happened to me!" Lauren cried. "Who *was* the creature that grabbed me? Did Jeff see it?"

"No, I was the only one who saw it, besides the kids," said Carmela. "They got so scared that they all ran screaming into the cabin, before Jeff ever showed up."

"Ohhh, Carmela, I am so freaked out," Lauren said with a shudder.

"Why don't you take a shower? It might help you relax," Carmela suggested.

"Yeah, I guess that's about all I can do right now," said Lauren. "My whole body aches."

While Lauren was in the shower, Carmela called Ms. Lawson on the cabin phone.

"Lauren is back," she told the director. "She was in the woods and sorta got lost, but she's okay."

Carmela doubted anyone was still searching for Lauren anyway. Ms. Lawson believed Lauren was in the camp somewhere, hiding out so she wouldn't have to face the music for the hoax.

In the morning, Carmela, Jeff, and Lauren wrote letters of apology to Ms. Lawson and Mr. Webb. But all morning, Carmela kept wondering if a monster had really grabbed Lauren. Was it the same monster that had grabbed her hair? Or was the monster really Lauren herself, in makeup and her body wrapped in dark clothes? But why would Lauren grab Carmela? Carmela was so confused!

All the teen counselors took their campers on a long mid-morning hike. Carmela was determined to be such an excellent counselor for the rest of the week that Ms. Lawson would forget all about the hoax. She didn't want to jeopardize her job or a good recommendation for future jobs.

The counselors and the kids walked through a canyon where pink granite rose on either side of the trail. Carmela had studied the rocks in this area, and she explained the appearance of any new type of rock as they walked.

"You see that black rock with veins of white? That's hematite," she said to her group. "It might look a little reddish. *Hematite* means 'bloodlike.' "

Later on, Carmela pointed out some beautiful rose quartz and howlite. "Howlite is a calcium silicate," she explained. She went on about the natural phenomena of the area.

But Carmela could not get that horrible-looking creature who attacked her and supposedly dragged off Lauren out of her mind.

As the three counselors sat eating lunch at a scenic point of interest, Carmela asked, "Did either of you guys talk about our hoax plans to anyone?"

"Well, yeah," Jeff admitted. "I talked a little bit about it with some of the other guys. I sorta told them what we were gonna do."

"You idiot," Lauren snapped. "We were supposed to keep it a secret!"

Jeff shrugged as he swalllowed a bite of his sub sandwich. "I didn't see any harm in telling the guys. They all promised to keep quiet about it," he said.

"Jeff," Carmela said, "one of those guys must have figured it'd be fun to get in on the joke, so he dressed up like a monster too. But then he got out of control."

"Yeah, and tried to drag me into the woods. He got really rough with me," Lauren said. "You and your big mouth, Jeff. If we could've done the hoax like we'd planned, then it wouldn't have blown up like it did."

Carmela watched Lauren's face closely. Was it all an act? Or did that terrible incident really happen to her? Did she see the other counselor pretending to be a monster and decide to play it up for attention? Or did some guy carry the joke too far and really try to drag her off?

Carmela knew that Lauren lied sometimes. Carmela had never totally trusted Lauren, even as young kids. She never lied about anything big, but sometimes Lauren could stretch the truth pretty far.

But would she lie about something this serious?

"How do we know the other monster was one of the teen counselors?" Jeff asked. "It could've been anybody. Maybe it was some nut who lives in the mountains. Maybe Don Clay didn't die after all, and he's still lurking around."

"But, Jeff," Carmela said, "don't you think it's a really weird coincidence that while we're pulling off our hoax with a guy in monster makeup, another prankster shows up looking the same way? I can't believe there's not a connection. If Don Clay were around, he would've shown up at a different time, and he wouldn't have been all made up like a monster. And why would he have run off so quickly? Why didn't he drag me off while he had the chance?"

Lauren nibbled on a cookie and stared off into the distance. "Did everybody know I was missing? Did Vance know?"

"I don't think anybody knew but Jeff, the adult counselors, and me," Carmela said.

Lauren looked disappointed. "Oh. I thought maybe somebody might've told Vance. You know, yesterday afternoon, he actually talked to me a lot. He wanted to know all about me. He was really attentive." A faint smile touched Lauren's lips. "I think he's sorta . . . you know, interested in me."

Carmela saw Jeff give Lauren a look. It was something like disappointment. Maybe he was thinking the same thing as Carmela.

She didn't say anything, but she saw the longing in Lauren's face. Lauren desperately wanted a boyfriend. Maybe, Carmela thought, she pulled the disappearing act to impress Vance in some way. Maybe she wanted to appear to be in danger to bring out whatever chivalrous instincts he had.

Carmela was more confused than ever.

6 As the counselors finished their lunch, Ms. Lawson and Mr. Webb approached them. They had driven up the mountain to deliver the drinks for the campers and counselors. "We received your letters," said Ms. Lawson. "We appreciate that you're apologetic about what happened. We'll just let it drop. We know you had good intentions, that you wanted to make this week memorable for the children. And you didn't do anything actually harmful. But we need to be sure nothing like that ever happens again."

"It won't," Jeff said.

"Thanks for understanding," said Carmela.

"And," Mr. Webb said pointedly, looking right at Carmela, "we are not going to repeat that far-fetched tale about two monsters, are we? Some of the children are claiming they saw two monsters, but I'm sure that's just the power of suggestion. There was just one monster, and it was you, Jeff, in that ridiculous makeup. We don't want our campers carrying home tales that they were besieged by hordes of monsters!"

"But there really was someone or something else," Carmela said stubbornly. "I won't talk to the kids about it, but there was. I know what I saw."

Both Ms. Lawson and Mr. Webb looked very unhappy at the comment. "If you did see another person with silly makeup on," Ms. Lawson said, "it was no doubt another of the teen counselors who wanted to get in on the very stupid prank. Now listen carefully. You are not to discuss this with any of the campers. We want no more talk of monsters or of some old hermit who used to live around here or anything of the sort. Is that quite clear?"

"Yes," Jeff said. The girls agreed too. When the two directors left, though, Lauren said grimly, "I'd sure like to know who that jerk was who attacked me!"

Just then, Vance sauntered over. He glanced at Jeff and Lauren and then smiled at Carmela. "You look great today," he said, looking her up and down.

"Oh, thanks," Carmela said. For Lauren's sake, she didn't make anything of the compliment.

"Did you hear about all the excitement last night?" Lauren asked.

"No, what happened?" Vance asked.

"We planned this little hoax to give the kids some excitement," Jeff explained, "but then this other jerk—nobody knows who it was—appeared all made-up and butted in on our hoax. Everything went downhill from there."

Vance laughed. "Did the kids freak?" he asked.

"Yeah," Carmela said. "They were screaming, and they ran into the cabin. It was awful."

"And you know what the worst part was?" Lauren chimed in. "This monster tried to drag me into the woods, and I barely got away from him. He was made up sort of like Jeff, and I thought it was Jeff, but then I realized it wasn't."

Vance looked at Lauren, a half-smile on his face. "Are you serious?" he asked.

"Dead serious," Lauren said. "I've never been so scared!"

Vance laughed at that. Just then Judy and Kandace began yelling. "I guess I'd better see what's going on," Lauren said. She gave Vance another quick smile and then ran off to see what all the excitement was.

"I'd better check on my guys too," Jeff said. "I can't take my eyes off them for a minute."

Carmela was left alone with Vance.

"You know," Vance said in a cruel voice, "that must have been a pretty desperate monster to grab Lauren. If it were me in that monster suit, and I wanted to drag someone off into the woods, it sure wouldn't be her."

Carmela felt her cheeks turn warm. Vance was leering at her, and she didn't appreciate it. At first Carmela thought that Vance was very good-looking, and she didn't mind all of his attention. But the more she talked to him, the more she thought he was just an insensitive jerk.

"Well, it's not really something to joke about, Vance," she said curtly.

"I know," Vance said, a little apologetically, "but I can't quite buy that story that Lauren is telling. It seems as if she wants to be the center of attention, and I kind of suspect nothing like that really happened to her."

Carmela noticed that Lauren had come back then. She was standing only a few feet from them. Carmela wasn't sure if she'd heard what Vance said, but she seemed to have a strange look on her face.

"What was going on?" Carmela asked.

"Nothing," Lauren said. "The girls were just afraid of a little lizard. I just told them to move away from it."

Then Lauren turned her attention on Vance. "So, Vance, when you're done with camp, what are you doing for the rest of the summer?"

"Last summer I worked at a car wash," he said.

"A car wash!" Lauren almost sneered. "Wow, I'm so glad I'll be in Acapulco. Poor thing!"

Carmela figured that Lauren probably *had* heard Vance's remark. This was her revenge, rubbing it in what a great rest of the summer she was going to have.

"Well, I guess that's how the rich live," Vance said.

"You know," Lauren said, "last summer Dad hired two high school guys to do yard work for us. Anyway, we all got to be friends, and they ended up coming to Acapulco with us. It's too bad you don't do that kind of work, Vance, or maybe you could come to Acapulco after all. We're building a water garden, waterfall, and rock-lined stream in our backyard."

"That sounds like hard work," Vance said.

"I bet you could handle it easily," Lauren said, "as strong as you are."

She was still trying to make a play for Vance. It made Carmela sad to realize that Lauren was so desperate to get something going with Vance that she'd dangle a job and the summer in Acapulco before him, even at the cost of her pride.

"I think I'll pass on that," Vance said.

"Okay," Lauren said crossly. "Enjoy washing all those dirty cars all summer!" Lauren tossed her head and walked off.

"Man, what a witch," Vance said when she was gone. "She thinks that just because she's rich she can have anything she wants. Well, I got news for Miss Moneybags. She's gonna need more than vacations in Mexico to get a guy like me. I don't go for cows."

Carmela was surprised at how bitter Vance sounded. "You know, Lauren is my best friend, and I don't like it when you call her names," she snapped.

"I hate people who come from money," Vance said.

"Well, maybe you need some help then, Vance, because you're a jerk," Carmela said.

"Wow, what a loyal little friend you are," said Vance. "Feisty too. I like that. I bet you're not rich like Lauren, are you? I bet your family lives in a little shack, just like mine. Maybe your old man isn't an alcoholic like mine is, but I bet your father drives an old car that makes a lot of noise, and I bet he sweats blood when the cost of gas goes up."

"My folks aren't rich, but it's not Lauren's fault. She's very generous with her friends, and she doesn't flaunt her money to me," Carmela said.

Vance drew a little closer to Carmela. "Did you know that you've got the most beautiful eyes I've ever seen?" he said.

"I don't want to hear this. I gotta go," Carmela said. Vance reached out and briefly held her wrist. "I sure hope we get to see each other after camp ends."

"I don't think so," Carmela said, pulling free of his grasp. "The girls are hiking, and I have to catch up."

"Carmela," Vance said, "I'm not some poor loser who can't show you any good times. I've got a rich uncle who's gonna die real soon, and he's leaving me some money. I'll be able to buy a really cool car and have some great times. You're welcome to share them."

Carmela felt like laughing, but she didn't. She didn't believe for a minute that Vance Putnam actually had a rich uncle about to give him tons of money from the grave. Carmela ran to catch up to her girls already back on the trail.

Carmela began pointing out birds and reading from her notebook. "There's a horned lark, you guys. Those hornlike tufts go away in the winter. Listen—do you hear the high-pitched song? That's how the males sing in the summer."

"Are they looking for girlfriends?" Kandace asked.

All the girls giggled at that, and then Judy said, "I think that cute boy you were talking to is looking for a girlfriend too, Carmela!"

Lauren was up at the head of the group, but Carmela was sure she had heard Judy's comment. Lauren seemed to walk even faster and hit the ground even harder with her walking stick.

Late that afternoon, everybody gathered back at camp to roast hot dogs and hamburgers and sing along with a group of college students who came in to entertain the campers. Lauren sat down next to Carmela.

"I totally hate Vance Putnam," Lauren said with savagery.

Carmela slowly ate her hot dog and said nothing. She didn't know what to say.

"He's hitting on you big time, isn't he?" Lauren asked. "Even the kids are talking about it. Every time he comes near you, his eyes bug out and he starts drooling."

"I don't even like him," Carmela said.

"Wow," Lauren said, leaning back on the grass, her hands behind her head. "It must be wonderful to have every guy you see dying to go out with you and being able to pick and choose. I've always envied you so much, Carmela. Sometimes I've even hated you because it comes so easy for you."

"Oh, Lauren, don't be stupid. You act like I'm some supermodel or something. I don't go out with that many guys," Carmela said.

Lauren sneered. "Erik Asbury stares at you in history, and in English there's John Cherry and Les Twombley," Lauren recited, moving on quickly to chemistry before Carmela could stop her.

"Lauren I don't even go out with those guys!" she said.

"But you could," Lauren said. "They all watch you going down the hall. Sometimes I stand there and watch how their gazes follow you. I think, wow, what would it be like to be so pretty?"

"You're pretty too, Lauren," Carmela said.

"Oh, please! Even my own parents tell me I'm not that attractive, and so I have to develop my personality and other qualities to attract a husband when I'm ready to marry. Like guys are attracted to personality! My mom is a big, strong woman, and I take after her. All the women in my family are big and . . . plain!" Lauren groaned.

Carmela felt terrible. She didn't know how to make Lauren feel better. The more she argued with her, the worse it got. Trying to convince Lauren that she was pretty sounded very hollow and hypocritical.

"Oh, I'll be able to snag a boyfriend," Lauren said. "Dad will let it be known that the poor schmo who marries me gets all the perks of being a Woodham son-in-law. That'll work. But I'll always know the guy didn't fall in love with *me*, that it was a package deal that was too good to pass up."

"Lauren, stop talking like that," Carmela pleaded. "It isn't even true."

"You know what?" Lauren said, sitting up and wrapping her arms around her knees. "I'd like to be that hideous monster that came out of the woods. Just for a little while. I'd grab all the jerks who've ever turned me down, and I'd knock their heads together. And then I'd like to add a hundred pounds to every pretty, skinny girl in the whole world!" Lauren's voice trembled with hurt and anger.

For this moment at least, Carmela could believe that Lauren *was* the second monster. Maybe jealousy and frustration had driven her to rush from the woods and yank on Carmela's hair just to frighten her . . .

7 Carmela was looking forward to getting some sleep that night. She hadn't slept much the night before, and she just wanted to forget about her troubles with Lauren for a while. She could tell that her campers were tired from hiking all day too. So it wasn't very hard to convince them to get their pajamas on, brush their teeth, and jump into their sleeping bags. She was right behind them.

Carmela had been sleeping for several hours when she was awakened by Lauren.

"What's the matter?" Carmela asked sleepily as she heard Lauren get out of bed.

"There's something out there," Lauren whispered.

Carmela sat up, frightened and suddenly very awake. "What do you mean?" she whispered back.

Lauren was at the window, parting the curtains.

Carmela jumped out of bed and ran to Lauren's side. "What is it? What did you see?"

"That thing or person or whatever. That monster. It must have run back into the woods," Lauren said, whispering rapidly between gasps of emotion. "It was looking in the window! I heard it scratching on the glass!"

Carmela stared out into the empty darkness. "You sure? You weren't just having a nightmare, were you?" she asked.

"No. It woke me up, scratching at the window. Then I heard it. It was calling my name!" Her whisper was nearing the point of waking up the campers. "Don't you see what's happening? It's a hoax to torment me! Some guy is dressing up in that makeup and pretending to want me. Isn't that just hilarious? Other girls have cool guys hanging around wanting to go out with them, but me, I've got a monster with bloody hair and a face that's half bone and half flesh. That's the kind of guy Lauren Woodham rates. Don't you get it?"

"What's happening?" one of the girls asked from her sleeping bag.

"Why's everybody talking?" another girl said groggily.

"Shhh," Carmela said quickly. "Go back to sleep. It's okay." Carmela grabbed Lauren's arm and pulled her into the bathroom. She didn't want all the girls to wake up. She turned to Lauren and whispered, "If some stupid guy is playing tricks like that, just ignore him. He'll get sick of it real fast if you just ignore him."

"No," Lauren said firmly. "This is so fun for this guy that he's going to keep it up for the rest of the week. It's like the story of my life. Remember that one really tall guy at Cleveland who looked like Frankenstein's monster? All he needed was the screw in his neck. Remember when he had a crush on me our freshman year? Everyone made fun of us. They used to draw cartoons of us, 'the world's ugliest couple.' "

Suddenly Lauren stopped talking and stared at Carmela. "You're having trouble keeping a straight face, aren't you? Because this really is funny unless you're the person the joke is on."

"Don't be ridiculous, Lauren," Carmela stammered.

"Oh, I can just read your mind, Carmela," Lauren seethed. "You pity me so much that you don't dare laugh. Poor, poor Lauren who never could get a real boyfriend is now being pursued by a monster. That's got to be just hilarious. Well, I'm going out there to find the jerk who's skulking around. Then I'm going to tear that stupid mask off his stupid face!"

Even though it was the middle of the night, Lauren threw on some sweats and a jacket and marched to the cabin door.

"No, Lauren," Carmela pleaded, "what if the guy in the costume is some dangerous psycho who wants to hurt you?"

"I wouldn't put it past Vance to be the one who's out there," Lauren said, her mind clearly made up. "He is such a dirty little jerk. I can imagine him hatching this idea and then laughing his head off with all his slimy friends."

Lauren opened the door and stepped outside. She shouted, "Hey, creep, where are you? Are you too much of a coward to show yourself?"

"Why did Lauren go outside?" Kandace asked. All the girls were stirring now, and

Carmela quickly closed the door. She turned to her campers and said, "Lauren just wants to look at the stars. She's gone out there to see the Big Dipper." She knew it was a lame excuse, but it was the middle of the night, and she couldn't think of anything much better.

"Can we go out and see it too?" Kiley asked eagerly, half out of her sleeping bag.

"No, not tonight," Carmela said. "Go back to sleep."

Carmela was frightened at the idea of Lauren being out there in the darkness with some unknown person. But at the same time, a thought was gnawing at her. She had a gut feeling now that Lauren *was* the monster. Carmela hadn't heard any scratching at the window. Only Lauren had heard it. True, Carmela was sleeping very soundly, but still, she had never actually seen Lauren and the second monster at the same time.

She wondered if she should call the adult counselors about Lauren being outside now, but she was afraid that would get Lauren in trouble. Carmela knew that if Lauren were just letting off steam, it would be better for her to remain calm and quiet.

She decided to wait, believing Lauren would return before very long. Lauren will probably stomp around the woods and let her anger cool, then she'll come back and be okay again, Carmela thought.

But Lauren did not come back. Half an hour passed, and then an hour. Carmela grew more worried by the minute. What if there *was* somebody out there, somebody dangerous? Maybe it wasn't just a guy counselor playing a dirty trick on Lauren like she had said. Maybe there was a strange person wandering around in the darkness. Maybe Lauren had walked into his hands and now was in danger!

What was it Jeff had said, half-jokingly, half-seriously? Carmela tried to remember. *We shouldn't be messing around with stuff like this. Half-dead, half-alive zombies wandering around . . .*

Maybe Don Clay was still alive, lurking around the mountains, Carmela thought. They said he probably died in the wilderness, but maybe he didn't. Maybe that second monster was some enraged and dangerous man angry at the people of Camp Roadrunner . . .

Carmela ran to the window and stared out into the darkness.

"Lauren," she whispered. "Where are you?"

Carmela's imagination began to run away with her. Had a crazed Don Clay come down from the mountains, and now did he have Lauren? Or was Lauren playing a crazy game?

Finally, after an hour and 45 minutes, Carmela couldn't wait any longer. She called Ms. Lawson. It was 2:00 in the morning. In five minutes Ms. Lawson appeared at the cabin door, and Carmela stepped outside to talk to her so they wouldn't disturb the girls.

"What's going on?" Ms. Lawson asked. Her hair was messed up, and she was wearing sweats. Carmela could tell that she had disturbed Ms. Lawson from a deep sleep.

Carmela explained everything that had happened that night.

"Do you see what has happened?" Ms. Lawson asked in an angry voice.

"No, not exactly," Carmela admitted.

"Lauren Woodham is a disturbed young woman," Ms. Lawson explained. "This is all an elaborate effort on her part to get attention. The other night when you and your friends decided to pull this hoax, Lauren disappeared then too, didn't she? Then she returned with some fantastic story. She liked the attention, and now she's done it again."

"I don't know," Carmela said. "I'm just worried—"

"Well, when Ms. Woodham comes waltzing back after another fictitious encounter with some mythical monster, we shall call her parents to come get her," Ms. Lawson interrupted, anger flashing in her eyes. "We cannot have some irresponsible young woman as a counselor here."

Carmela almost believed what Ms. Lawson was saying. But there was a part of her that still didn't quite believe it.

"Ms. Lawson, did you ever hear of a man named Don Clay who lived around here?" Carmela asked suddenly.

Ms. Lawson looked perplexed. Then

she said, "Yes, of course. He was one of those rabble-rousers who took it upon himself to decide what is best for society, and heaven help anyone who disagrees. Some years ago when we first opened Camp Roadrunner, he was quite active, but then he disappeared. Everyone said he must have died. Why? What has Don Clay got to do with all this?"

"Oh, I don't know," Carmela said. "I keep thinking of that second monster I saw. I mean, what if it was some outsider who came to cause trouble?"

"Carmela, don't be ridiculous. What is happening here has nothing to do with an ancient mountain man who has long since died. For goodness sakes, are you irrational too? You think Don Clay is roaming around looking in cabin windows? Is that what you are suggesting? Honestly, when I was your age, I was a serious, dependable young woman, not some child with a runaway imagination!" Ms. Lawson stormed.

"It's just that I've known Lauren for a long time, and it's hard to believe she would lie this much," Carmela said.

"Go back to bed," Ms. Lawson demanded. "The girls are getting restless wondering what's going on. Their sleep is being disturbed. This is unacceptable. Now, good night!"

Carmela went back into the cabin and quietly climbed into her bed, but she couldn't sleep. She kept tossing and turning and worrying about Lauren. Up until this camping trip, Carmela had never realized how unhappy Lauren was, how jealous she was of Carmela. Maybe, Carmela thought, I've been so wrapped up in my own life that I've been insensitive to Lauren's feelings.

The camping week had brought it all to a head. Spotting Vance had been the last straw. Lauren had so wanted him to notice her, and instead he was drooling over Carmela.

As dawn lightened the sky, Carmela crawled out of bed and stared out the window, searching for Lauren. She didn't care anymore what crazy story Lauren would bring back, she just wanted her to be okay. Then, when Lauren returned home, she and her family would be going to Acapulco, and that would cheer her up.

Lauren always said she loved the Mexican people, that they were warmer and more real than most of the students at Cleveland High. Maybe, Carmela thought hopefully, this year Lauren will meet a nice guy down there who will make her summer extra-special. Carmela hoped that would happen. She really cared about Lauren, and she wanted her to be happy.

But as the red dawn painted the sky, there was no sign of Lauren. Another teen counselor was assigned to Carmela to help her with the girls. And at 8:00 Carmela was called to the camp office. When Carmela got there, Jeff was already seated in the office. Carmela noticed that he looked really upset. Ms. Lawson and Mr. Webb were there too. They looked like somebody had died.

Carmela had never felt such a sense of anxiety.

"This dreadful hoax you people thought up has had terrible consequences," Mr. Webb said. The tall, nervous-looking man looked as if he were about to cry.

"Why? What's happened?" Carmela asked in a breaking voice.

"Apparently, some sick person picked up on your little stunt and decided to take it further," Ms. Lawson said.

"What's happened?" Carmela demanded, her voice trembling. "Has something happened to Lauren?"

"Lauren is still missing," Ms. Lawson said, speaking very deliberately, "but some distressing evidence has been spotted about a hundred yards from your cabin. The police are on their way."

8 "What?" Carmela gasped. "What evidence? Is Lauren hurt or what?"

"There is evidence of a struggle," Mr. Webb said tersely. "That's all we can say. We want you to proceed with your day as usual. There is nothing to be gained by upsetting the children. When the police arrive, we'll call you in to talk to them. This is really terrible. Nothing like this has ever happened at Camp Roadrunner."

"Nothing," Ms. Lawson agreed sadly.

As Carmela and Jeff walked out together, Carmela said, "You don't think something bad has happened to Lauren, do you? She thought some guy in terrible makeup was playing a joke on her, and that's why she went out and looked for him last night."

"I still wonder if Lauren just messed up the scene to make it look like something had happened," Jeff said. "I don't know. Lately, she's really seemed miserable. It's too bad. She's so fun." Jeff looked down at his feet and kicked at a pinecone. "A couple of times, I wanted to ask her out, but then I figured she wouldn't want to go out with me."

Carmela turned and looked at Jeff in surprise. "Did you ever *tell* Lauren how you felt?"

"No way," Jeff said. "I didn't want to mess up our friendship."

You should have told her, Carmela thought. Oh, you should have!

Carmela spent the morning working on an art project with her girls. They were painting a butterfly mural on the side of the physical education building. The girls were laughing and talking in the bright morning sunshine, but all Carmela could think about was Lauren.

All of a sudden, another counselor came running over toward Carmela's group. "Carmela, you're supposed to go to the office," she said. "I'll watch your girls."

Carmela's legs were weak as she walked toward the office. She figured the police were there. She dreaded what the police might say or not say.

"Hey, Carmela, wait up," Vance said, suddenly running up beside her. "There's a police car over by the office. What's going on. Do you know?"

"Lauren's missing," Carmela said.

"Did she run off or something?" Vance asked, walking briskly to keep up with her.

"I don't know. She's just missing. I'm really worried," Carmela said.

Vance reached over and gave Carmela's hand a squeeze, "Hey, don't worry your pretty little head," he said.

Carmela stopped and faced Vance. "Vance," she said in disgust, "she's my best friend, and I care about her, okay?"

"Ahhh, she just took off," said Vance. "I knew when I first met her that she was a psycho. She's got what the shrinks call issues. I could tell that. She's pretty pathetic. Didn't you hear her trying to lure me into going out with her by dangling that trip to Acapulco in front of me? That's pretty sick for her to be so pushy, don't you think?"

"She's just lonely," Carmela said. Another police car arrived, and she watched it park beside the first one. Her heart sank still further. They must have found some really ominous evidence of foul play, she thought. She glared at Vance. "Just leave me alone, okay? I've got to go in there and talk to the police." She started walking again.

"Uh, oh. You were the last person to see her, huh?" Vance said with a wry grin. "Maybe they think you girls got into a cat fight or something. Take it easy, babe. Don't let them pressure you into saying anything they can use against you."

Carmela threw Vance a bitter look as she opened the door to the office. She did not think Vance was even the least bit good-looking anymore. His personality was too disgusting.

When Carmela walked into the office, Ms. Lawson and a police officer were waiting for her.

"Carmela, this is Sergeant Agnes Alvarez," Ms. Lawson said. "She's here to investigate what happened to Lauren. Sergeant, Carmela Masters is a good friend of Lauren's, and she was the last person to see her before she disappeared last night."

Carmela was nervous, more nervous than she could ever remember being. She sat down opposite the sergeant.

"What's happened to Lauren?" Carmela asked. "Nobody has told me anything, except that some evidence was found. You think there was a struggle?"

"We are trying to find out what happened to Lauren," Sgt. Alvarez said. "We understand she got up in the middle of the night because she thought someone was playing a joke on her by scratching on the cabin window?"

"Yes, that's right," Carmela said. "Lauren went out to yell at the guy she thought was harassing her, but she never came back."

"Lauren is a very excitable girl, and there is a strong possibility that she is playing some kind of grand hoax on us with this disappearance," Ms. Lawson said.

Carmela shot Ms. Lawson an angry look. No one seemed to be taking Lauren's disappearance seriously except her.

Sgt. Alvarez questioned Carmela for about 30 minutes until she was interrupted by the ringing of Ms. Lawson's phone. The look on Ms. Lawson's face instantly changed from anxiety to great relief. "Oh, this is wonderful news," she said. She put down the phone and said, "That was Mrs. Woodham, Lauren's mother. She has been contacted by her daughter. Apparently, it was a runaway situation after all, just as we suspected."

The phone call changed everything. Sgt. Alvarez asked a few more questions, and then she closed her notebook and left with the other officers. The tension was gone. Lauren Woodham was all right. Her own mother had said so.

"I'm so glad Lauren isn't hurt or anything," Carmela told Ms. Lawson. "I was so scared."

"We were frightened too," Ms. Lawson said, letting her guard down in relief after finding out Lauren was all right and some violent tragedy had not struck Camp Roadrunner. "Lauren's jacket was found in the brush. It was ripped, and there were even some spots of blood in the weeds. It looked as if she had been kidnapped and was injured in the struggle. All sorts of terrible possibilities went through our minds. What a dreadful event to mar the outstanding reputation of Camp Roadrunner. I was devastated!"

Carmela was dismissed from the office. When she stepped outside, she saw that Vance was waiting for her. "What happened?" he asked.

"Lauren's mother called and said she's okay," Carmela said.

"Hey, that settles that then," Vance said. "You know, I've got news too. My rich uncle is sinking faster than they expected. I might be coming into my inheritance really soon. A hundred thousand. And I can play the stock market on the Internet and turn it into much more. I'm telling you, Carmela, I'm gonna be on top of the world."

"You know," Carmela said, "it's kinda sick that you have a relative who cares enough about you to leave you money, and you're acting like a vulture, circling around and waiting for him to die."

Vance looked hurt by the comment. "Why do I get the feeling that you don't like me very much, babe?" he asked.

"Maybe because it's true, Vance. I like people with a lot of heart, and that doesn't describe you." With that, Carmela turned sharply and walked toward her cabin.

Carmela was relieved that Mrs. Woodham had called to say Lauren was all right, but Carmela was still anxious to hear her friend's voice for herself and find out what had really happened. So when she got inside the cabin, she decided to call the Woodham house. She dialed the number she knew by heart. She let it ring quite a few times, but there was no answer.

She and Jeff had a two-hour break after lunch, so they mounted bicycles for a ride around Camp Roadrunner, using the scenic bike trail that wound around the lake.

"I tried to call Lauren, but nobody was home. I still wonder why she ran off like that," Carmela said.

"Yeah," Jeff said. "She sure scared everybody."

"I wonder if she's actually at home or if she's staying with friends," Carmela said.

They came to a ranger station and public campground. They parked their bikes and walked into the store to buy some bottled water.

"There's a telephone," Carmela said. "I think I'll try to call Lauren again. I just want to hear her voice, and then I'll be able to relax."

Carmela dialed the Woodham house. She was not only anxious to hear Lauren's voice, but she wanted to know what had happened the night before. Did Lauren have a confrontation with one of the guy counselors?

The phone barely rang once before it was picked up on the other end. Carmela recognized the voice as that of Lauren's father.

"Yes?" Mr. Woodham almost barked into the phone.

"Hi, Mr. Woodham, this is Carmela. I was really worried about Lauren. Is she there? I'd like to talk to her," she said.

"No," he said, "she's not here right now. We're very busy, Carmela. I can't talk now." Mr. Woodham's voice shook. He was usually a very calm man, but now he sounded almost hysterical. Carmela was shocked.

There was something wrong!

"Mr. Woodham, Lauren is okay, isn't she?" Carmela asked.

"Get off the phone, David!" Lauren's mother yelled from the background. "For heaven's sakes, don't tie up the phone!"

"I have to go," Mr. Woodham said.

Carmela went numb with fear. "But Mr. Woodham, I'm so scared. Is Lauren in trouble or something?" Carmela asked.

But the phone line had already gone dead in her ear.

Jeff appeared outside the phone booth, bottled water in hand. "What's the matter? Is something wrong?" he asked as he saw the shock on Carmela's face.

"I called Lauren's house and talked to her father. He sounded awful!" Carmela said. "Now I'm scared all over again, Jeff. I thought everything was okay, but Lauren must be in some kind of trouble!"

"Wow, maybe her parents are mad at her for leaving camp like that. It sounds like she's gone off the deep end," Jeff said. "I guess maybe we should've been better friends to her and noticed stuff going wrong." Jeff shook his head sadly.

"Yeah," Carmela said, feeling guilty too.

"I bet she's still missing. She probably called her mom to say she was okay, but I bet she hasn't come home. I bet her mom lied to the police just so there wouldn't be trouble over her being a runaway. They probably want to work it out themselves."

"Yeah," Jeff said, "rich people are sometimes scared of bad publicity. Lauren's dad is a big CEO. He probably wouldn't want it on television that his daughter is a runaway."

"Maybe Lauren is just hanging out with friends. She had a couple of friends at Cleveland who were kind of different. They were pretty wild and partied all the time. Maybe that's all her parents are upset about. I mean, Lauren never had problems with her parents, so maybe they're just freaking over this," Carmela said.

The pair biked around the lake and then turned to go back to Camp Roadrunner. Suddenly Jeff said, "You know, let's stop and look at the place where Lauren disappeared. I know the cops looked at it and everything, but I'd feel better if I saw it myself."

"Good idea," Carmela said, touched

that Jeff had brought it up. He was really worried about Lauren. He was as worried as Carmela was.

Carmela and Jeff biked to the beginning of the walking trail, about a hundred yards from the cabin. "Ms. Lawson said that Lauren's jacket was found in the brush. It's not there anymore. I guess Ms. Lawson got it to mail back to the Woodhams. And the police must've taken samples of those blood spots. Lauren could have just stumbled and scratched her knee on something," Carmela said.

"Weird, though. Why would she throw down her jacket and not go pick it up? Or even if it got caught on a branch or something, I don't see why she'd just leave it there," Jeff said.

"Yeah," Carmela agreed. "It gets chilly in the mountains at night. Why would she just leave her jacket on the ground?"

"Maybe she saw this monster guy that she thought was taunting her, and they had a fight or something," Jeff said. "Maybe it grabbed her jacket. Then she ran . . ."

"But then wouldn't she have come back for it?" Carmela asked.

"Maybe he grabbed her, and she couldn't go back," Jeff said, his eyes wide with alarm.

"But, Jeff, when he was gone, I mean, why didn't she get her jacket *then*?" Carmela asked.

Jeff and Carmela looked at each other, the fear growing. "Something's not right, Jeff," Carmela said.

"Yeah, but Lauren's mom said she was okay," Jeff pointed out. "She loves Lauren. She wouldn't have called off the police if Lauren was still missing and might be in danger. I mean, it doesn't make sense, right?"

"No, it doesn't," Carmela said.

"Lauren is probably mad at the world. She's mad at us, and she's mad at her parents, and maybe she just tossed her jacket in defiance of everything. Maybe she did it because she wanted everybody to be upset. Maybe it was like a cry for help," Jeff said.

"Yeah, because we weren't very good at listening before, huh? Oh, wow, Jeff, I wish I'd helped Lauren more when she was feeling bad," Carmela said.

"Me too," Jeff said. "I wish I'd asked her out when I wanted to. I sort of thought she'd turn me down, so I didn't take the risk. Big-shot Jeff Lyman didn't want to risk a little rejection."

"I think she would've said yes, Jeff," Carmela said.

Carmela knelt down in the brush and stared at the mashed-down weeds. "Jeff, it looks as if somebody rolled around here. Look at how the weeds are broken down . . ." she said.

"Yeah, but that doesn't prove anything," Jeff said.

"I know," Carmela said. "I bet Lauren is okay, and she's just hanging out somewhere to get even with all of us for neglecting her." Carmela wanted to believe that. It was the most consoling explanation. It was less scary than the other alternatives—that for some reason Lauren was still in danger, but her parents were trying to help her without outside interference.

"Carmela," Jeff said, "look, there's something kind of glittering here."

Carmela hurried to where Jeff was pointing. It looked like something had been ground down into the soft earth. Carmela stooped and pried out a charm bracelet.

"Jeff! It's Lauren's charm bracelet! She loves it so much. It has a charm for each year of her life. It was from her dad. She *never* took it off. She never would've thrown that away," Carmela said. "Oh, you don't think something horrible happened, do you? That a bear or something came through here and . . ."

Jeff grabbed Carmela's hand and pulled her gently to her feet.

And then he hugged her tightly.

9 "Carmela," Jeff said, "you've got to remember that Lauren's parents said she's okay. They must know that. Otherwise they wouldn't have called off the cops, right?"

Carmela nodded. She had to cling to that. But she was not completely reassured. So when they got back to Camp Roadrunner, Carmela placed another call to the Woodham house. This time she got Lauren's mother.

"Mrs. Woodham, I hate to bother you again, but I'm so upset about Lauren. If I could just talk to her for a minute, then I'd feel okay," Carmela said.

"Everything is fine, Carmela, but Lauren can't talk to you right now," Mrs. Woodham said, sounding very tense. "I promise you that Lauren will call you when . . . it is . . . right for her."

"Mrs. Woodham, is Lauren sick? What's happening? Can't you tell me what's happening? Lauren is my best friend, and

I'm just so worried," Carmela said.

"Carmela, listen to me. Lauren is fine, but she's very . . . upset. If you care about her, you will not bother us again. Please, please do not call this home again. It is very important that our phone line remain open. Lauren will call you when all this is settled. But, Carmela, please, you are endangering Lauren by calling her and tying up the phone . . . because the . . . uh . . . doctors and the . . . people caring for her might call at any moment. Good-bye now."

Carmela stared at the dead phone in her hand as she had done before. Maybe the Woodhams were embarrassed that Lauren had some sort of nervous breakdown and needed to be hospitalized.

All Carmela was sure of was that Lauren was not okay. Something was terribly wrong.

When Carmela walked out of her cabin to find her group, Vance came walking up, a big smile on his face. "So, one more day with the little monsters, eh? Then we're free," he said. "Are you looking forward to the grand finale tomorrow? The hot dog roast, the sing-alongs, all the rowdy little savages kicking up their heels."

"I'm still worrying about Lauren," Carmela said. "I can't think of anything else."

"Look, let the crazy babe do her thing, whatever it is. And don't forget the money I'm coming into and all the fun we can have if you're up for it," Vance said.

"I'm not interested," Carmela said coldly. "I'm going to be very busy working at camp this summer."

"Look, my aunt is not gonna last much longer, Carmela. I could get that hundred thousand next week. Can you imagine spending a hundred thousand dollars?" Vance said.

Carmela stared at the young man in surprise. "Vance, the last time you talked about the will you said it was your *uncle* who was dying. Now it's your aunt? What's with you?" Carmela asked.

Vance looked flustered for a minute, but he recovered quickly. "Look, I made a mistake. I misspoke, that's all. Haven't you ever made a mistake? It's my uncle," Vance said. "The important thing is, I'm gonna have lots of money."

"If it's even true that your poor relative is dying, people don't just hand out the money the day he dies. They send the wills to court, and lawyers argue and all that stuff. It could be years before you see any of that money. But even if you got the money tomorrow, I'm still not interested in seeing you this summer or any other time."

"You'll be sorry, babe," Vance shouted after Carmela as she walked away. "You're missing out on more fun than you've ever dreamed of. While you're sweating away here at camp, I'll be surfing the waves in Hawaii."

Carmela caught up with her kids at the sand volleyball courts. The campers were scheduled to play volleyball and tennis this afternoon. Carmela talked to the counselor who had taken over for Lauren to find out what she had missed while on break. Then Jeff joined Carmela while his boys assimilated with the girls for a coed game.

"Did you call the Woodhams?" Jeff asked.

"Yeah. Mrs. Woodham told me Lauren

would call me when she could, but I shouldn't call anymore because I was tying up the phone, and important calls were expected. She sounded totally drained. I don't know what to think," Carmela said.

***

The next afternoon Carmela and Jeff had another couple of hours off while the other counselors took the campers swimming. It was the last day of camp, and the campers always got to vote on their favorite activity to do again. More often than not, swimming was chosen.

"Jeff, are you up for hiking in the woods and just looking around?" Carmela asked after delivering her girls to the on-duty counselors.

"Yeah, sure, but what are we looking for?" Jeff asked.

"I don't know," Carmela said. "I just think there's something out there that'll tell us something about what happened to Lauren."

Carmela and Jeff hiked down the walking trail from the place where

THE MONSTER IN THE MOUNTAINS

Lauren's jacket was found. They began walking slowly.

"I looked in the camp library and found a book that talked about local characters," Jeff said. "There was stuff in there about that guy, Don Clay. It had pictures of him and everything. He was a big, menacing-looking guy. He had quite a few run-ins with the local authorities over trees they were cutting down, stuff like that."

"How old would he be now if he were still alive?" Carmela asked.

"About 63," Jeff answered.

"Wow, that's not very old," Carmela said.

"He built himself a log cabin right in these mountains," Jeff went on. "He took a long time to build it because he wouldn't let anybody help him. The book said it's still standing somewhere around here. But maybe it's fallen apart by now. The book is about 20 years old, I guess."

They continued walking. There was still plenty of light. They had brought flashlights along, and each carried a first-aid kit and Swiss army knife in their backpacks in case anything came up.

"Carmela!" Jeff said suddenly. "There's a building up ahead. You see it through the trees?"

"Yeah," Carmela said.

They walked faster to reach the building. It turned out to be a roughly hewn log cabin. It appeared to be in good condition. Jeff said, "I read that Don Clay would never cut a tree, even to build the cabin. He only used wood from trees that had already fallen, cut down by lightning or infested with disease. That's why it took him so long to finish it too . . ."

"How did he die? Did it say anything about that in the book?" Carmela asked.

"No," answered Jeff. "He was hale and hearty when the book came out. He was only in his forties, I guess. But somebody at Camp Roadrunner, a handyman who's been there for ages, told me that Don Clay was sick one summer. He went into the mountains as usual, but then when spring came, he didn't come down for supplies. The locals sent people up to check the cabin, but there was no sign of him."

"He probably died out in the

wilderness, huh?" Carmela asked.

"Yeah. When he complained of being sick, his cronies told him to see a doctor, but he was a stubborn guy, and he said he didn't trust doctors. He said he'd probably not see another spring, and he didn't mind. He said he wanted to die lying on a bed of pine needles with a starry sky above his head. He told the guys that he didn't mind the wild things taking care of his remains. He said that was the way of nature, and he wanted to go that way," Jeff said.

They drew closer to the cabin.

"It's a really cool-looking little cabin," Carmela said. "Looks snug."

"I wonder if the door is locked," Jeff said. "He was leasing the land from the government, so they probably own it now."

They approached the cabin cautiously, and Carmela reached out to try the doorknob. The door sprang open at once. "Wow, it's open," Carmela said. She looked at the inside of the cabin. It was messy and almost bereft of furniture. It looked as if it had been a home to passing hikers for many years.

"Ugh, it looks messy," Carmela said. "Food wrappers, soda cans."

Jeff walked in first. "Lots of papers on the floor," he said. He stooped and picked up one of the newspapers. "Look, this is from the day before yesterday. It's the comics. So somebody was hanging out here recently."

Suddenly they heard a thumping sound. It sounded like wood hitting wood.

"What's that?" Carmela asked.

"If it's a woodpecker, it must be an awfully big one," Jeff said.

"Get serious," Carmela scolded. "Where's that sound coming from?"

"From here," came a familiar voice. Carmela and Jeff turned. They saw Vance standing in the doorway. He was hitting the door frame with a walking stick. "What are you guys doing snooping around my home away from home?"

"What are *you* doing here?" Carmela asked.

"Ah, Matt and I are buddies," Vance said. He pointed at another guy, standing nervously behind him. Carmela recognized Matt Klein as another counselor from camp. Vance continued explaining. "We found this cabin, and sometimes when we get time off, we sneak out here and have a few beers. You know what old Lawson and Webb would do if they caught us drinking."

Matt disappeared out of Carmela's view.

"How long have you been using the cabin?" Jeff asked.

"Since we got here," Vance replied. "Matt was a counselor here last year, and he found it. It used to belong to some crazy old hermit."

Carmela heard the strange thumping sound again. But this time it wasn't Vance.

"That's Matt," Vance said with a smile. "He's collecting pinecones. Some store in town buys them and then paints them for Christmas. Sometimes you gotta knock 'em down."

"You shouldn't take pinecones from a national forest," Carmela said. "They're seeds for the next generation of trees."

"Man," Vance said, "don't be such a straight arrow, Carmela. It's really boring."

Carmela stared hard at Vance. *Liar* was written all over his face. The strange thumping sounds were something else, something sinister. Carmela didn't know what it was, but she felt sure of her hunch.

"Come on, Jeff," Carmela said sharply, grabbing Jeff's arm. "Let's get out of here." She was anxious to get Jeff alone so she could share her suspicions with him.

"You guys," Vance said, "don't rat on me back at camp. Don't tell Lawson and Webb about our little pub up here. Otherwise, I'll give her an earful about some of the stuff you guys have been doing."

"That'd be lies, right?" Jeff asked.

"Lies? Sure, why not. Just don't rat on us. Matt and I need to veg out here," Vance said.

Carmela and Jeff walked away from the cabin. Carmela's heart was pounding. When she was sure they were out of earshot, Carmela said, "Jeff, do you think—"

"Something's going on back there, yeah," Jeff cut in.

"That thumping sound," Carmela said. "It sounded as if it were coming from under the cabin. In a crawl space or something. Don Clay probably had a fruit cellar or something down there to preserve his food."

Jeff nodded, his face turning grim. "Carmela, it almost sounded like somebody down there trying to attract our attention. Like somebody . . . being held hostage under the house. Maybe tied up and gagged with no way to make sound except by kicking at the floor or the wall . . ."

Carmela felt her legs go numb. She grasped the branch of a tree to steady herself. "Lauren? Oh, Jeff!" she gasped.

"I'm not saying it's Lauren, or *anybody*. But it sounded like somebody trying to get our attention, and the explanations Vance gave sounded really hollow," Jeff said.

"Jeff, do you think maybe Vance kidnapped Lauren and is holding her for ransom?" Carmela asked.

"Lauren really went overboard talking about how rich she was, going to Acapulco in the summer and stuff. That might have triggered a plan in Vance's mind," Jeff said.

"We don't have to be back at camp for an hour and a half," Carmela said. "Let's hide in the woods and just watch the cabin for a while. Maybe we'll see something that will give Vance away."

"Okay," Jeff agreed. They took their places, well hidden by brush. They had a clear view of the cabin.

Matt appeared in the clearing before the cabin. Carmela remembered seeing him at Camp Roadrunner and wondering why the camp had hired such a jerk. He was impatient with the kids, and twice Carmela heard him cursing at them. He seemed like a weasel.

Carmela could tell that Vance and Matt were talking, but they were too far away for her to understand what they were saying.

Vance turned then and went inside the cabin. Matt stayed outside, looking around, occasionally glancing into the woods. He looked as if he were expecting to see something.

"I hope he's not looking for us," Jeff whispered. "That might be what they were talking about. Maybe our faces gave it away that we didn't believe them."

Matt walked around the edge of the

woods, but he never came close to where Carmela and Jeff were hiding. Then Vance came outside again, and they talked animatedly. Matt went around the side of the cabin, and the next sound Carmela and Jeff heard was a motorcycle motor. Matt rode his motorcycle across the dirt in front of the cabin and then down to the road. In a second he was gone.

Vance stood outside the cabin, drinking. He went back in then and closed the door.

"Matt won't make it back to camp when all the counselors go on duty if he's heading for town," Carmela said.

"Carmela, I don't think he cares," Jeff said.

Jeff took a deep breath then. "Carmela, wait right here. Don't move. I'm going to move in a little closer. I think I know what's going on, but I want to make sure," he said.

Carmela reached out and grabbed Jeff's arm. "Don't go any closer, Jeff. It's too dangerous," she pleaded. She really cared about Jeff, whether as a friend or something more. It didn't matter. She couldn't imagine anything happening to him.

"I've got to," Jeff said, giving Carmela's hand a squeeze. "I have to find out if what I think is happening really is."

Carmela trembled as Jeff inched closer to the cabin. He crouched down about ten yards from the cabin and listened. From where she was, Carmela could barely hear the thumping sounds coming from inside the cabin. On impulse, Carmela left her hiding place and joined Jeff. When Jeff saw her, he frowned and whispered, "Keep down."

Carmela lay on her stomach next to Jeff and listened.

"I think Matt probably went to some rendezvous spot to get the ransom money," Jeff whispered. "That's the inheritance you said Vance was talking about. There's no dying uncle. He and Matt are holding Lauren for ransom."

"He must've been wearing that monster makeup when he kidnapped her that night," Carmela said. "She probably doesn't even know who kidnapped her! Poor Lauren. Down in that cellar! That's why her parents acted so weird. They were dealing with the kidnappers, and they figured if the police got involved, it could endanger Lauren."

But Carmela and Jeff weren't absolutely sure.

Until the next second.

Carmela figured that Lauren must have somehow gotten the gag from her mouth. Instead of thumping sounds, her scream came from the cabin. It was a muffled scream from deep in the cellar, but Carmela knew it was Lauren's voice.

"I can't breathe down here! You've got to give me some air!" the voice cried.

Vance disguised his voice when he answered her. He growled in a low grunt. "Shut up. Your parents are sending the money. Shut up until I get the money. You better shut up or you'll never get out of there alive."

"Ohhhh," Carmela groaned, near tears.

Vance returned to his post outside the cabin, pacing.

"We've got to get back to camp and call the police," Jeff whispered.

Carmela and Jeff turned and began

crawling through the brush as close to the ground as they could. They couldn't risk being seen. But, as careful as Carmela was, she caught her shoulder on a branch and it snapped, making a sharp sound.

Vance quickly looked out into the woods. "Somebody out there?" he shouted as he moved into the clearing. "Who's out there?"

Carmela and Jeff exchanged horrified looks.

Jeff motioned with his eyes, and he and Carmela scooted behind a fallen tree.

Through a crevice in the log, Carmela could see Vance. He was walking around the clearing. After about five minutes, Carmela figured he must've convinced himself that there was no one around. He grabbed another can of beer from a cooler.

Then Lauren screamed again.

Carmela looked at Jeff and shuddered. They had to hurry. Lauren was in serious danger. If she made too much trouble, who knew what Vance might do?

Vance went inside. Carmela heard him pound on the cellar's trapdoor with a heavy object, maybe a shovel. "You shut up," he growled in his disguised voice. "You shut up, or I'll make it so you don't ever talk again!"

Then Vance appeared outside again.

This time he had a gun.

10

"We gotta go," Jeff said urgently. They began moving through the brush again. Jeff led the way, and Carmela followed just behind him. Carmela carefully pushed aside the twigs and shrubs so she wouldn't make any more noise. But they needed to make better time than this if they were going to help Lauren. It was more than two miles back to camp.

"Soon as we're a little farther, we can get up and run," Jeff whispered.

But as Carmela and Jeff scrambled through a bed of dried leaves, a swarm of nesting birds flew out of the trees, making a din.

"He's looking this way," Carmela cried.

Vance, gun in one hand, started in the direction of Carmela and Jeff.

"We've gotta make a run for it," Jeff cried.

The pair jumped to their feet and

sprinted as fast as they could toward Camp Roadrunner.

But Carmela knew that Vance had seen their figures darting ahead through the trees.

"I'll go west," Jeff gasped. "I'll try to lead Vance over there toward the stovepipe mountains. You double back and see if you can reach Lauren."

Carmela nodded. She was desperately afraid for Jeff. But he was on the track team. He had a good chance of outrunning Vance. Carmela clung to that hope as she started to double back toward the cabin.

Carmela was breathing so hard that she felt as if there were a huge hand on her chest, squeezing her heart and her lungs. She heard the sounds of Jeff crashing through the brush with Vance chasing after him. Carmela ran still faster, gulping air. Finally she was there. She ran into the cabin and knelt on the floor over the trapdoor.

"Lauren, are you okay?" Carmela cried.

"Carmela! Thank God!" Lauren sobbed in a muffled voice.

Carmela yanked open the trapdoor and shone her flashlight beam down. It was little more than a crawl space, and Lauren was bound hand and foot, a blindfold over her eyes. The gag she had finally spit out was a wet rag around her chin.

Carmela scrambled down the three steps leading into the cellar. She jerked her Swiss army knife from her backpack and began sawing at Lauren's bonds. She got Lauren's arms and legs freed, then Lauren pulled off the blindfold.

"Where's Jeff?" Lauren asked. "I heard Jeff's voice too."

"He's leading Vance away from here, toward the stovepipe mountains. He's in trouble. Vance has a gun, and if he catches up to Jeff . . ." Carmela groaned.

Lauren climbed from the dark crawl space with Carmela's help. Her legs were stiff at first from being bound for so long.

"Oh, Carmela, he kept that costume on and spoke in that fake voice when he was letting me drink some water or something, but I knew right away it was Vance! The minute he grabbed me, I knew, but I didn't let on that I knew because then I think he would've killed me."

Outside, the two girls stared off toward the stovepipe mountains. They didn't know exactly where Jeff had led Vance, but if they were running, Jeff had probably stayed pretty close to the trail. So the girls started down the same trail.

Then, suddenly, they heard a gunshot.

"Lauren," Carmela cried, "he's shot Jeff! He caught up to Jeff and shot him!"

Lauren and Carmela grabbed each other's hands and ran as fast as they could toward the sound of the shot. They jumped over fallen trees and ran through briars, ripping their pants.

They heard shouts then.

"That's a granite wall you're up against, man," Vance said. "You've got nowhere to go. You'd better come out."

"Not a chance," Jeff shouted back.

Carmela looked at Lauren with relief. Vance must have fired that shot trying to flush Jeff out.

"Come and get me," Jeff taunted.

But in spite of Jeff's bravado, Carmela saw that Vance had chased him into a box canyon. The only way for Jeff to escape was straight up the mountain behind him, and Vance would spot him in a minute. It would be like hitting a fly on the wall.

"We've got to creep up behind Vance," Carmela whispered.

Lauren nodded. Her face looked ferocious.

They followed the shouts of the young men taunting each other.

"You're not ruining my plan, man," Vance said. "No little peon like you is going to ruin the best plan I ever had."

Sooner or later Vance would reach Jeff. Carmela knew there was no contest between a guy with a gun and one with nothing but a Swiss army knife.

"Come on," Carmela whispered. They were across a small creek from where Vance crouched. If they splashed through the water, it might alert Vance, and he could turn and fire at them.

Lauren grabbed Carmela's arm. "You cut around over there, and I'll come from the other direction. I think we can step on rocks crossing the creek. He can't shoot at both of us if we're that far apart," she said.

Carmela nodded. She was trembling with fear, but Lauren looked fearless. She seemed almost eager for the confrontation. Her teeth glittered as her lips rolled back over her teeth.

Carmela watched Lauren climb a boulder just over the creek. Shrieking, she hurled herself at Vance's back. Carmela watched Lauren knock Vance off his feet and send the gun in Vance's hand skidding across the dirt. Carmela reached the spot in one desperate dash, kicking the gun away as Vance grabbed for it.

Carmela stooped and grabbed the gun. She had never held a gun in her hands before. She didn't know the first thing about them. But she held it in her trembling hands and yelled at Vance, "I've got you covered!" She borrowed the line from some movie she had seen long ago.

Lauren had leapt on Vance like a mountain cat, bringing him down. Her big, athletic body was a match for Vance's. She straddled him as he lay facedown in the dirt. She seized a handful of his hair and yelled, "You stupid jerk. You are going to jail for such a long time that you'll be on

Social Security when you get out!" Then she gave his hair a yank, causing him to grunt in pain.

"That's for putting on that costume, luring me from the cabin, roughing me up, and kidnapping me, loser!" Lauren said.

Then she gave Vance's hair another painful pull. "That's for leaving me tied up in that dirty cellar crawling with rats," she said.

Carmela saw Jeff appear out of the box canyon. He stared in awe and then admiration at the sight of Carmela holding the gun and Lauren straddling a shaken Vance.

Lauren gave Vance's hair one final jerk, almost pulling a tuft of it out by its roots. "And that's for worrying my poor parents and putting my friends in danger!"

A big grin spread across Jeff's face as he climbed down from his hiding place and stood next to the girls. "Is she awesome or what?" he asked Carmela as he stared at Lauren.

Carmela handed Jeff the gun, and the trio marched Vance back to Camp Roadrunner. When Carmela called the police, Vance confessed that Matt was going to pick up the ransom money. Lauren called her parents, who wept with relief at the news that she was safe and out of danger.

Carmela, Lauren, and Jeff drank hot chocolate and waited for their parents to come and get them. They were excused from the last night at camp because of the ordeal they had been through.

"Carmela," Jeff said between sips of hot chocolate, "do you remember when we had California history last year and we read how California got its name?" There was a goofy smile on his face that she had never seen before.

"Yeah," Carmela said, "California was an island in some novel. It was ruled by some fierce Amazon queen named Calafia. I remember. So what?"

Jeff continued to grin. "Remember how it described Queen Calafia? Didn't it describe her as strong, virtuous, valiant, and beautiful?"

"Yeah, so?" Carmela asked.

"So?" Lauren echoed, her lower lip quivering.

Carmela suspected she knew what Jeff was driving at.

"Doesn't Lauren remind you of her?" Jeff asked, looking at Lauren shyly.

Lauren's eyes widened in surprise. Then a shy but genuine grin spread across her face.

"Thanks, I guess," Lauren said.

"Maybe . . . maybe you know . . . we could go out sometime when we get home. Just you and me. You think?" Jeff asked.

Lauren smiled. "Sure, yeah. That'd be great," she said, flushing.

Carmela beamed at how happy her two friends looked. She had never been so happy to lose a potential boyfriend.

The headlights of the Lyman, Masters, and Woodham family cars snaked up the mountain and came upon Camp Roadrunner, along with police cars with red lights flashing on their roofs.

As Carmela hurried toward her parents, she turned once and looked back. Jeff had his arm around Lauren. Carmela ran on, relieved, happy, and swearing to herself to never take part in another hoax.